THE LAST DAYS OF TONY MACBRIDE

CASE FILES: POCKET-SIZED MURDER MYSTERIES

RACHEL AMPHLETT

SAXON
PUBLISHING

THE CASE FILES SHORT STORY
SERIES

THE LAST DAYS OF TONY MACBRIDE

THE LAST DAYS OF TONY MACBRIDE

As I hear the opening bars of music spew from the organ, I know I'm in trouble.

The key is one I can't sing – I've either got to squawk like a crow or do my best Johnny Cash impression, and neither is going to go down well with the woman in the front pew, her hand shaking as she holds the service programme for her husband's funeral.

She knows every word, of course. We're both regular churchgoers, but her visits are from a sense of religious fervour and guilt.

My visits come with the job.

My name is Allan O'Reilly, owner of O'Reilly and Sons.

Funeral director.

It's an unimaginative business name, but I inherited it from my dad so it's not like I had any choice in the matter.

I clear my throat and join in with the chorus, my voice little more than a murmur. At least my lips are moving in time with everyone else, even if the minister gives me a sideways look that tells me he's not convinced.

The caterwauling reaches an uneven crescendo. The congregation battles with the organist, who is intent on wrenching every last note from his instrument of torture until he finishes, and we fall back into our seats, exhausted with the effort.

As they sit, I reach into my collar and scratch at the label in my shirt that has been tickling my neck for the past ten minutes. It's newly purchased, especially for this occasion.

I try to make an effort for my clients.

I hear my name, and the minister gestures to me. It's my turn.

I fix a benevolent smile on my lips and begin to read the eulogy for Miriam MacBride's husband.

I wrote it myself.

It took me three late nights and half a bottle of dark rum, but I got there in the end.

I glance up.

Miriam is staring at me.

My voice falters and I clear my throat while the minister rests his hand on my arm and tells me to take my time.

I try not to snort out a manic laugh at the absurdity of it all, the effort causing my eyes to water, and then that sets everyone else off. The people in the front row are dabbing their cheeks with paper tissues, a few muffled sobs reaching my ears.

You see, I knew Tony MacBride.

Better than most.

A large man, his suits could have burst from his

frame if not for the handmade quality of the material and a generous cut to the cloth.

Tony knew how to invest, how to spot an opportunity – and how to hold a grudge.

He began his working life selling used sports cars. The garage wasn't far from here, in a nondescript town that carried the stench from the local abattoir across its rooftops most days in August. A hardworking man, he had the gift of the gab and a network of acquaintances who could get things done.

Tony soon gained a reputation as a man who could fix things.

The garage expanded over time to include a service workshop, tucked around the back of the low-slung property so as not to detract from the gleaming vehicles in the showroom that faced the road.

Me and my mates used to peer through those showroom windows on our way home from school, shielding our eyes as we drooled over the cars we could never afford and would never drive.

Three days after my sixteenth birthday, I got a part-time job at the garage. I was scrawny then, a mere scrap of a lad but Tony saw something in me and gave me a chance.

I swept floors, sorted the stock of spare parts, and soon found myself apprenticed to an elderly mechanic with a shock of nicotine-tainted white hair.

I loved the scent of grease and motor oil, the clamour of eighties pop songs blaring on the radio competing with the clang and clatter of tools upon metalwork. On Fridays, I'd help in the spray booth wearing a mask against the paint fumes, watching and learning as the experts worked.

Within two years, I'd qualified and taken over additional duties.

Tony would wander out from his office to the service bays for the important jobs, the ones involving less prestigious vehicles but requiring as much care and attention to detail.

These were the cars that arrived in the small hours, under cover of darkness and a tarpaulin.

He would place his suit jacket on a hanger that could always be found on a hook behind his office door, then roll up the sleeves of his shirt and stand, arms folded over his chest while we toiled through the night.

He trusted the men who worked for him, trusted their workmanship at turning something like a blue four-door family saloon into a red version of a model two years older, all within twenty-four hours.

Then, another acquaintance of his would arrive to take the vehicle away, a man who stayed in the shadows and kept his face from prying eyes. He would return two days later with a fat envelope, the contents of which would be divided among us once Tony took his share.

In the summer months, Tony would close the garage early on a Friday afternoon, tie an apron around his waist and hand out cold bottles of beer while a barbecue hissed and spat sausage fat outside the doors of the service area.

We'd play cricket then, the sound of the willow bat against a leather ball echoing off the walls, Tony umpiring with gusto.

At Christmas, his bonuses were generous. He'd take us to one side to check everything was okay at home, at work, in life.

You see, Tony valued loyalty above everything else.

Insisted on it.

Demanded it.

He knew my dad, too.

They'd been friends at school since the age of six and Dad would often peer into the service bays to greet me before disappearing into Tony's plush office, shutting the door behind him. Every now and again, raucous laughter would filter through, and then Dad would emerge once more, Tony slapping him on the back in farewell.

Tony spent a lot of time behind that closed door, making his deals, planning his next investment.

Miriam would sweep in every now and again – a blast of expensive perfume followed by a jangle of gold jewellery and a swish of silk. She wouldn't stay long, just enough to make her presence known, get her bank account topped up with another cheque from Tony, and then off she'd totter in her six-inch high heels to the shiny new cabriolet parked at the kerb.

In my younger days, I'd fantasise about her – until Tony took me to one side and left me with no illusions what would happen if I tried anything.

He loved her it seemed, despite her faults.

Everything changed when my Dad died, and I took over the running of his business.

I kept in touch with Tony over the years, our

paths crossing from time to time as the need arose – nothing more, nothing less.

The garage continued to offer repairs and sales by day and kept a busy trade in alternative services by night. Local councillors extolled Tony's exuberance for employing the town's youth, especially those who might have otherwise shunned work for other nefarious activities.

And Miriam continued to flirt with the new apprentices.

I inhale the scent of fresh flowers filling the front of the church.

Lilies, of course and then the carnations – always a favourite of Tony's and a permanent fixture in his jacket buttonhole no matter the season or day of the week. Someone has ordered lilacs, a dark contrast to the white roses woven into the wreath with ivy tresses.

Arranged around the threadbare russet-coloured carpet below the flower display are white envelopes – cards of condolence that weren't posted to the house, and donations to Tony's favourite charity for greyhound rescue.

I blink and raise my gaze from the piece of paper in my hand.

At least forty pale faces peer at me, some craning their necks to get a better view.

As the curtains sweep closed, shielding the coffin from view and the first notes of Puccini's *Nessun Dorma* are broadcast over our heads, Miriam MacBride weeps loudly, lamenting her loss. She turns to the woman next to her – her sister – and proclaims her undying love for Tony.

It's a shame Tony's not around to see it all.

He'd be tickled pink.

You see, Tony MacBride is now Martin Broadshaw, and currently en route to Malaga.

His wife is oblivious to the fact that the man she's been having an affair with for the past year is now being whisked towards the furnace instead, dead these seven days past, the victim of a blow to the back of the head with a cricket bat.

I can still feel the weight of the willow bat, still hear the wet thud as it met his brain.

Like I said, Tony MacBride demands loyalty.

He knows how to hold a grudge.

And he has a network of acquaintances who can get things done.

THE END

ABOUT THE AUTHOR

Rachel Amphlett is a USA Today bestselling author of crime fiction and spy thrillers, many of which have been translated worldwide.

Her novels are available in eBook, print, and audiobook formats from libraries and retailers as well as her website shop.

A keen traveller, Rachel has both Australian and British citizenship.

Find out more about Rachel's books at: www.rachelamphlett.com.

ALSO AVAILABLE IN THE CASE FILES SERIES

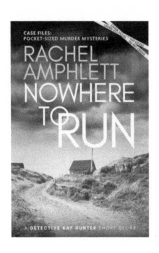

Nowhere to Run

When a series of vicious attacks leaves the local running community in shock and fear, probationary detective Kay Hunter is thrust into the middle of a fraught investigation.

ISBN eBook: 978-1-913498-68-9

ISBN paperback: 978-1-913498-69-6

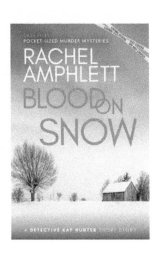

Blood on Snow

A suburban housewife is found dead in her garden. There is no weapon, no witnesses, and the only set of footprints belong to her cat.

Probationary detective Kay Hunter and her colleagues are convinced it's murder – but how can they find a killer when there are no clues?

ISBN eBook: 978-1-913498-70-2
ISBN paperback: 978-1-913498-71-9

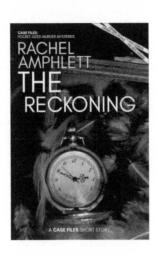

The Reckoning

The newest arrival at a care home for the elderly carries an air of mystery that even an ex-WW2 Resistance fighter can't help trying to solve.

Then matters take a sinister turn…

ISBN eBook: 978-1-913498-70-2
ISBN paperback: 978-1-913498-71-9

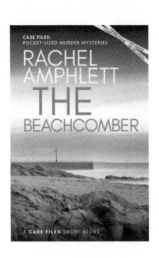

The Beachcomber

Staying at a tiny guesthouse in Cornwall after the summer, Julie spends her days combing the beaches, looking for things to collect while hiding from her past. Then a storm breaks, and suddenly she's scared.

Because you never know what might wash up after a storm...

ISBN eBook: 978-1-913498-93-1
ISBN paperback: 978-1-913498-94-8

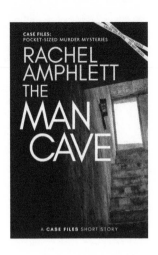

The Man Cave

When Darren regains consciousness in a dank
basement, escape turns out to be the least of his
worries...

ISBN eBook: 978-1-913498-96-2
ISBN paperback: 978-1-913498-97-9

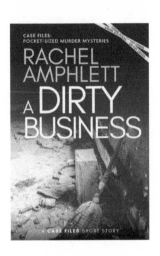

A Dirty Business

When Michael arrives at work early one winter's day, he discovers that he's not the only one who's had a busy morning...

ISBN eBook: 978-1-913498-98-6
ISBN paperback: 978-1-913498-99-3

Lightning Source UK Ltd.
Milton Keynes UK
UKHW010826031022
409835UK00004B/739